HOW TO SURVIVE...
CHRISTMAS CHAOS
WITH HORRID HENRY

Francesca Simon spent her childhood on the beach in California, and then went to Yale and Oxford Universities to study medieval history and literature. She now lives in London with her family. She has written over fifty books and won the Children's Book of the Year in 2008 at the Galaxy British Book Awards for *Horrid Henry and the Abominable Snowman*.

Tony Ross is one of Britain's best known illustrators, with many picture books to his name as well as line drawings for many fiction titles. He lives in Oxfordshire.

There is a list of **HORRID HENRY**
titles at the end of the book.

Also by Francesca Simon

Don't Cook Cinderella
Helping Hercules

and for younger readers

Don't Be Horrid, Henry
Illustrated by Kevin McAleenan

The Topsy-Turvies
Illustrated by Emily Bolam

HOW TO SURVIVE...
CHRISTMAS
CHAOS
WITH HORRID HENRY

Francesca Simon

Illustrated by Tony Ross

Orion
Children's Books

First published in Great Britain in 2011
by Orion Children's Books
a division of the Orion Publishing Group Ltd
Orion House
5 Upper Saint Martin's Lane
London WC2H 9EA
An Hachette UK Company

2

Compiled by Sally Byford from the *Horrid Henry* books
by Francesca Simon and Tony Ross.

ISBN 978 1 4440 0134 1

A catalogue record for this book is
available from the British Library.

Printed in Great Britain
by Clays Ltd, St Ives plc

www.horridhenry.co.uk
www.orionbooks.co.uk

CONTENTS

HELLO FROM HORRID HENRY

Christmas! Presents! Presents! Presents! Chocolate! Presents! More chocolate! Presents! All day telly! Presents!

That, of course, is how Christmas should be. No pesky relatives clogging up the sofa and hogging the telly, no horrible little brothers, and no sprouts EVER.

With my fool-proof, 100% tried and tested survival guide, you can have the Christmas YOU deserve, this year, and the next and the next...

No more bad presents. All the chocolate you want. Little brothers and sisters firmly in their box where they belong.

So what are you waiting for? Stop reading this and get plotting!

Henry

HORRID HENRY'S TOP CHRISTMAS MOTTOS

☆ Getting is better than giving.

☆ Save up your pocket money – then spend it on yourself.

☆ Worms don't get presents.

☆ Beware the wrinklies – currants, raisins and grandparents.

☆ Sprouts make you bald.

☆ Every present you buy means something you can't buy for yourself.

☆ I want … gets.

☆ Satsumas are NOT presents.

HORRID HENRY'S CRAFTY ADVENT CALENDAR

You will need

a large piece of stiff card
pencils, paints and felt tip pens
sticky tape
silver foil or coloured tissue paper
scissors
24 sweets or chocolates

Instructions

1. Draw a Christmas tree on a piece of cardboard and paint it green.
2. Wrap up sweets or chocolates in silver foil or coloured tissue paper.
3. Fasten the sweets to your Christmas tree picture with sticky tape.
4. Number the sweets 1 to 24 in any order, then enjoy a sweet every day until Christmas!

HENRY'S TIP: Remember, a big calendar means big sweets too!

CARDS TO RICH AUNT RUBY

Mum has written a letter to Aunt Ruby,
but Henry swaps it with a letter of his own.

Dear Ruby
We're all so looking forward to
having you and Steve for
Christmas this year. And
don't worry, Henry is delighted
to share his bedroom. I'm sure
the cousins will have loads of
fun together.
See you soon!
Love from your younger sister.

Dear Ruby

Sorry, no room here for you and Steve this Christmas. But drop off all your presents for Henry as soon as possible — no need to come in, just ring the bell and leave them at the door. He'd really like loads and loads and loads of cash. In fact, think of a huge sum, and then double it, to make up for the horrible lime green cardigan you gave him last year. And since there's no need to give Peter any presents, you can add his Christmas money to Henry's

Remember, Ruby, Christmas is all about giving so now's your chance to give give give to Henry

See you at Steve's next prison visit.

Your younger Sister

CONFUSED CHRISTMAS CARDS

Horrid Henry is the school Christmas postman. Can he deliver the right cards to the right people? Untangle the muddled-up names on each of the envelopes below.

1. GMAETARR
_ _ _ _ _ _ _ _

2. AILWMIL
_ _ _ _ _ _ _

3. PRHAL
_ _ _ _ _

4. RSM DBODOD
_ _ _ _ _ _ _ _

5. RREIUDGN
_ _ _ _ _ _ _ _

6. TBRE
_ _ _ _

CHRISTMAS CODE MESSAGE

Horrid Henry sends Ralph a secret code message in his Christmas card. Can you uncode Henry's message using the grid below?

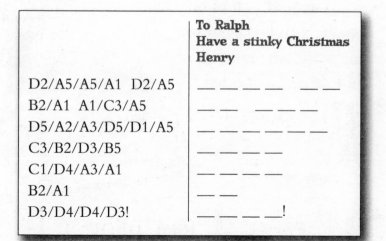

To Ralph
Have a stinky Christmas
Henry

D2/A5/A5/A1 D2/A5   _ _ _ _   _ _

B2/A1 A1/C3/A5   _ _   _ _ _

D5/A2/A3/D5/D1/A5   _ _ _ _ _ _

C3/B2/D3/B5   _ _ _ _

C1/D4/A3/A1   _ _ _ _

B2/A1   _ _

D3/D4/D4/D3!   _ _ _ _!

	1	2	3	4	5
A	T	U	R	K	E
B	Y	A	B	C	D
C	F	G	H	I	J
D	L	M	N	O	P
E	G	S	V	W	X

SURVIVING YOUR FAMILY AT CHRISTMAS

Pretend to be reading a book. Your parents will be so shocked they'll leave you alone. (Remember to hide a comic inside.)

Pretend to be deaf.

Hide in your
room with
your music
on full blast.

Do your chores so badly, and slowly, that
your parents won't bother you again.

END-OF-TERM SCHOOL SURVIVAL

Rehearsals had been going on forever. Horrid Henry spent most of his time slumping in a chair. He'd never seen such a boring play. Naturally he'd done everything he could to improve it.

'Can't I add a dance?' asked Henry.

'No,' snapped Miss Battle-Axe.

'Can't I add a teeny-weeny-little song?' Henry pleaded.

'No!' said Miss Battle-Axe.

'But how does the innkeeper *know* there's no room?' said Henry. 'I think I should—'

Miss Battle-Axe glared at him with her red eyes.

'One more word from you, Henry, and you'll change places with Linda,' snapped Miss Battle-Axe. 'Blades of grass, let's try again …'

Does Henry survive the School Nativity? Find out in 'Horrid Henry's Christmas Play' from *Horrid Henry's Christmas Cracker*.

CHRISTMAS PLAY CRISS-CROSS

Fit all the parts of the
School Christmas Play
into the criss-cross puzzle.

4 letters
MARY
STAR

5 letters
SHEEP
JESUS
GRASS
ANGEL

6 letters
JOSEPH
DONKEY

8 letters
SHEPHERD

9 letters
INNKEEPER

CLUE: Fit Horrid Henry's part into the puzzle first!

SURVIVING THE SCHOOL CHRISTMAS PLAY

When Miss Battle-Axe is giving out
the parts, shout very loudly –
'I WANT TO BE JOSEPH!'

Refuse to be a blade of grass –
it's the worst part.

Trick the leading actor into leaving the show.
Then offer to replace him.

If all else fails – make your own
part BIGGER.

CLEVER CLARE'S CHRISTMAS QUIZ

1. Postmen in Victorian England were sometimes called 'robins' because:

   (a) Their uniforms were red
   (b) Their noses were red
   (c) Their hair was red

2. The little sausages wrapped in bacon that we eat at Christmas lunch are called:

(a) Sausages in bed
(b) Pigs in a blanket
(c) Pigs' trotters

3. The first sort of Christmas pudding was like porridge and it was called:

   (a) Frumenty
   (b) Glop
   (c) Ready Brek

4. When should you take down your Christmas decorations?

(a) Never – just leave your mum and dad to do it
(b) 24th December
(c) 6th January

5. Nowadays mince pies are filled with:

- (a) Raisins and sultanas
- (b) Minced beef
- (c) Peanut butter and jelly

6. Why is Boxing Day so called?

- (a) A big boxing match was always held on that day
- (b) It was the day for sharing the Christmas Box with the poor
- (c) Little brothers and sisters should be put into a box for the day

Check out the answers on page 68.
What's your score?

Clever Clare says:

0–2 You're clueless about Christmas! Just like Horrid Henry, I bet you think it's all about presents.

3–4 You're quite clued-up, but maybe your brain is ready for a long rest over the Christmas holidays.

5–6 Happy Christmas! You're almost as clever as me!

SANTA'S GROTTO

'What do you want for
Christmas, Peter?' asked Santa.

'A dictionary!' said Peter. 'Stamps, seeds,
a geometry kit, and some cello music, please.'

'No toys?'

'No thank you,' said Peter. 'I have plenty of toys
already. Here's a present for you, Santa,' he added, holding
out a beautifully wrapped package. 'I made it myself.'

'What a delightful young man,' said Santa. Mum
beamed proudly.

'My turn now,' said Henry, pushing Peter off Santa's lap.

'And what do you want for Christmas, Henry?'
asked Santa.

Henry unrolled the list.

'I want a Boom–Boom Basher and a
Goo–Shooter,' said Henry.

'Well, we'll see about that,' said Santa.

'Great!' said Henry. When grown–ups said
'We'll see,' that almost always meant 'Yes'.

Does Henry get the present he asks for? Find out
in 'Horrid Henry's Christmas' from *Horrid Henry
Gets Rich Quick*.

PUZZLING PRESENTS

Solve the crossword clues and find out what
Horrid Henry and his family got for Christmas.

Across

2. Pimply Paul gave
   Prissy Polly this
   Megawatt
   Superduper tool
   for making holes
   in walls.

4. Another present for
   Polly – it's for
   putting flowers in.

5. Horrid Henry
   wasn't pleased with this present which is used for
   writing thank you letters.

6. Dad gave this to Mum to keep his shirts wrinkle-free.

Down

1. See 3 down for this clue.

2. Grandpa gave Granny this present to get rid of all the
   dust in their house.

3. This clue is in two words – the first word fits in 3 down
   and the second fits in 1 down. Mum's present to Dad,
   used for holding hot things when he's cooking.

PERFECT PRESENTS...

Loads and loads of cash

Robomatic Supersonic
Space Howler Deluxe

Boom-Boom Basher

Day-Glo slime

Terminator Gladiator
Fighting Kit

Bugle Blast Boots

Zapatron Hip-Hop Dinosaur

Strum 'N' Drum

Huge tin of chocolates

...AND HOW TO GET THEM

Smile nicely at your parents and say 'pleeeeease'.

If that doesn't work, scream and shout 'I hate you!'

Write to Father Christmas and tell him to give you what you want this year.

Ambush Father Christmas and hold him hostage with a Goo-Shooter.

Dear Father Christmas
I want loads of money and a ROBOMATIC SUPERSONIC SPACE HOWLER with all the attachments
Mum and Dad want me to have one too.
Henry
P.S. Peter has been horrible all year and deserves NO presents
Please give his to me

GUESS THE PRESENT

Horrid Henry has a tag-swapping plan to avoid the presents he doesn't want. Help him guess what's inside by matching the parcels to the list of presents.

BOW TIE

GOO-SHOOTER

ZAPATRON HIP-HOP DINOSAUR

CELLO

TERMINATOR GLADIATOR TRIDENT

SOCKS

SATSUMA

DICTIONARY

CATAPULT

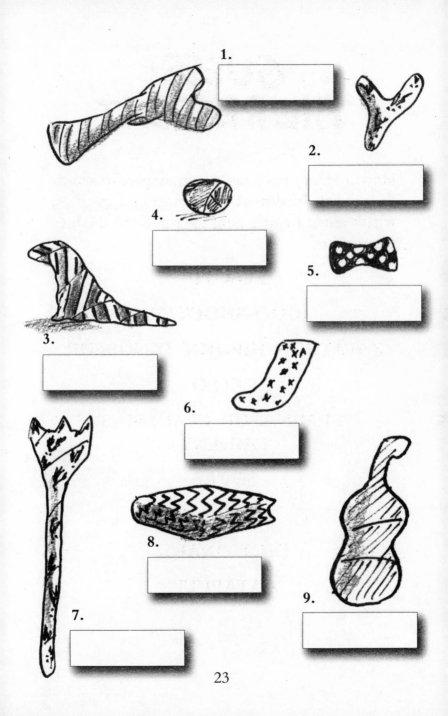

1.

2.

3.

4.

5.

6.

7.

8.

9.

23

WORST PRESENTS...

Lime-green cardigan

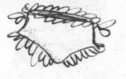

Pink frilly
lacy knickers

Socks

Satsumas

Dictionary

Baby Poopie
Pants Doll

...AND HOW NOT TO GET THEM

Sneak downstairs when everyone's asleep, and swap the present labels around.

Take the labels from your sock and Satsuma-shaped parcels and stick them on the Terminator Gladiator and Strum 'N' Drum-shaped ones instead.

Guess the shapes of the presents and hide the ones you don't want.

CHRISTMAS CLOCKWORDS

Horrid Henry swaps his most hated present for the chocolate bar in Perfect Peter's stocking. Follow the time instructions below to find out what it is.

Where does the big hand go when it's...

1. Half past five
2. Ten to six
3. Quarter past five
4. Twenty to six

5. Five past five
6. Twenty past five
7. Quarter to six

Answer: __ __ __ __ __ __ __

WHAT'S INSIDE?

Two parcels have arrived for Henry and Peter. Can you help Henry get the present he wants? In each of the boxes, cross out the letters that appear three times. Rearrange the remaining letters to find out what's inside.

L H x e L
a i O A
X i D A i
E h X E h

Answer: _ _ _ _

E R s y O
Y E y
R S E O L S
G y L r e

Answer: _ _ _

HOW TO SURVIVE THE THANK YOU LETTERS

Always tell your mum you'll write your thank you letters later…

…but if she says no TV till you've written them, try these sneaky tricks…

Make your handwriting as big as possible so it fills more space.

Write exactly the same letter to everybody.

Even better, write just one letter on the computer, like this:

> Dear Sir or Madam
>
> Thank you/no thank you for the
>   a) wonderful
>   b) horrible
>   c) disgusting
> present. I really loved/hated it. In fact it
> is the best present/worst present I have
> ever received. I played with it/broke it/ate
> it/spent it/threw it in the bin straightaway.
> Next time just send lots of money.
>
>   Best wishes/worst wishes
>
>   Your friend or relative

THANK YOU LETTER

Henry writes Rich Aunt Ruby a thank you letter with pictures to puzzle her. Can you work out what he's written?

WHO SURVIVES THE CHRISTMAS CRUSH?

Horrid Henry, Rude Ralph and Moody Margaret are determined to get Father Christmas's last pot of slime. Who survives the Christmas crush and wins?

Positions: 1st, 2nd, 3rd
Presents: Slime, Crayons, Sweets

	POSITION IN QUEUE	PRESENTS
HORRID HENRY		
MOODY MARGARET		
RUDE RALPH		

Clues

1. Moody Margaret gets pushed behind Rude Ralph in the queue.
2. Father Christmas gives the crayons to the 1st person in the queue.
3. Rude Ralph gets the sweets.

HOW TO AVOID SPENDING MONEY ON OTHER PEOPLE'S PRESENTS

Lend out your things as presents – you can take them back afterwards.

Make a sweet wrapper collage – you'll have to eat the sweets first!

Write poems for your
parents – when you're
a famous poet they'll
be proud to show off
your early work.

Find presents around
the house – soap in
the bathroom, a
cloth from the
kitchen, or a very
useful plastic bag.

Give away
unwanted
presents from
last Christmas.

CHRISTMAS TREE TRIUMPHS

'Right, who wants
to decorate the tree?'
said Mum. She held
out a cardboard box brimming
with tinsel and gold and silver and blue baubles.

'Me!' said Henry.

'Me!' said Peter.

Horrid Henry dashed to the box and scooped up as
many shiny ornaments as he could.

'I want to put on the gold baubles,' said Henry.

'I want to put on the tinsel,' said Peter.

'Keep away from my side of the tree,' hissed Henry.

'You don't have a side,' said Peter.

'Do too.'

'Do not,' said Peter.

'I want to put on the tinsel *and* the baubles,' said Henry.

'But I want to do the tinsel,' said Peter.

'Tough,' said Henry, draping Peter in tinsel.

'**Muuum!**' wailed Peter.

Find out if Henry gets his way in 'Horrid Henry's
Christmas Presents' from *Horrid Henry's Christmas Cracker*.

CHRISTMAS TREE WORDSEARCH

Can you find all the Christmas Tree words in the wordsearch?

FAIRY
TINSEL
BAUBLES
TREE
STAR
LIGHTS
BELLS
RIBBONS
BOWS
GARLAND
BERRIES
CONES

S	E	N	O	C	S	T	E	B
L	E	R	M	T	I	R	G	E
L	R	N	A	A	I	T	A	R
E	T	R	O	B	R	G	R	R
B	A	U	B	L	E	S	L	I
L	B	O	W	S	A	D	A	E
I	N	Y	R	I	A	F	N	S
S	T	I	N	S	E	L	D	A
T	O	R	S	T	H	G	I	L

The left-over letters reveal what Horrid Henry wants to put on the top of the Christmas tree:

_ _ _ _ _ _   _ _ _ _ _ _

SPOT THE
DIFFERENCE

1. _____
2. _____
3. _____

Can you spot the six differences between
the two pictures?

4. _____

5. _____

6. _____

HOW TO SNEAK THE CHOCOLATES OFF THE TREE

EITHER

Sneak down at night when everyone else is asleep.

OR

Offer to decorate the tree — and hide half the chocolates! You can sneak the rest later.

CHRISTMAS SUDOKU

All four squares, all four rows and all four columns must include one holly leaf, one bauble, one star and one candle. Can you solve it?

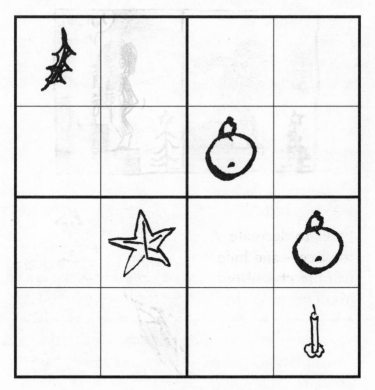

FATHER CHRISTMAS FUN

Horrid Henry lay on the sofa with his fingers in his ears, double-checking his choices from the Toy Heaven catalogue. Big red 'X's' appeared on every page, to help you-know-who remember all the toys he absolutely had to have. Oh please, let everything he wanted leap from its pages and into Santa's sack.

After all, what could be better than looking at a huge, glittering sack of presents on Christmas morning, and knowing that they were all for you?

Oh please let this be the year when he finally got everything he wanted!

Does Henry get everything he wants? Find out in 'Horrid Henry's Ambush' from *Horrid Henry's Christmas Cracker*.

HAVE YOU BEEN HORRID OR PERFECT THIS YEAR?

START → Have you called your brother or sister horrid names?

YES → Have you stuck your tongue out at your teacher?

YES → Have you sneaked any sweets from the kitchen?

NO (from brother names) → Have you done all your homework?

NO (from homework) → Have you been good at school?

NO (from tongue out) → Have you helped your mum and dad with the chores?

YES / NO (from sweets) → Have you eaten all your vegetables?

Have you done all your homework? **YES** → Have you kept your bedroom tidy?

Have you been good at school? **YES** →

Have you kept your bedroom tidy? **YES** → Have you washed your hands before meals?

Have you helped your mum and dad with the chores? **YES** →

Have you eaten all your vegetables? **NO** → Have you gone quietly to bed on time?

Have you eaten all your vegetables? **YES** →

Have you washed your hands before meals? **YES** → Have you gone quietly to bed on time?

Have you kept your bedroom tidy? **NO** →

Have you washed your hands before meals? **NO** →

Have you gone quietly to bed on time? **NO** →

Have you gone quietly to bed on time? **YES** →

You're as horrid as Horrid Henry. Don't be surprised if Father Christmas forgets to visit you!

You're as perfect as Perfect Peter. Father Christmas is sure to bring you a sackload of satsumas. Yum!

41

CRISS-CROSS CHRISTMAS JOKES

MARY	TOAD
PUDDLE	TROUSERS
SOOTS	TURKEY

1. Why does Father Christmas go down the chimney?

   Because it __ __ __ __ __ him.

2. Why does Santa wear bright red braces?

   To hold his __ __ __ __ __ __ __ __ up.

3. Who is never hungry at Christmas?

   The __ __ __ __ __ __ because he's always stuffed!

4. What is green, covered with tinsel and goes *ribbet ribbet*?

   Mistle- __ __ __ __ !

5. What do you call a snowman on a sunny day?

   A __ __ __ __ __ __ __

6. What is Father Christmas's wife called?

   __ __ __ __ Christmas.

Now fit the same six words
into the criss-cross puzzle
below.

CLUE: Start by fitting in
the longest word.

CRAFTY CHRISTMAS STOCKINGS

These stockings are perfect for hanging on the tree and stuffing full of sweets and chocolates!

You will need

felt
scissors
craft glue

narrow ribbon
decorations – sequins,
   glitter or beads

Instructions

1. Cut two stocking shapes out of felt.

2. Carefully glue the two pieces together at the edges, leaving the top open.

3. Fold your ribbon in half to make a loop to hang on the tree. Glue inside the stocking.

4. Decorate your stocking with sequins, glitter or beads.

5. When the glue is dry, hang your stocking on the Christmas tree.

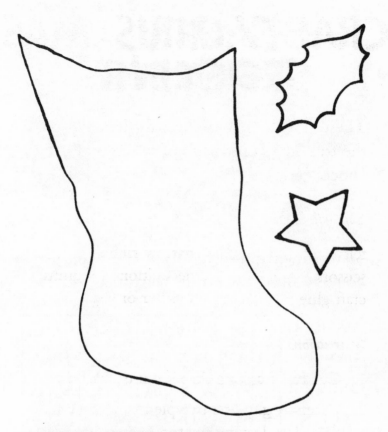

HORRID HENRY'S TIPS

Don't mess about with a little stocking –
make a great big giant one.
Write a big message on your stocking
to Father Christmas, so he can't miss it –
FILL THIS WITH MONEY AND CHOCOLATE.
NO SATSUMAS OR WALNUTS!

Henry

SANTA'S REINDEER

Settle down and solve this puzzle while you're waiting for Father Christmas.

C	H	U	V	T	G	P	O	R
O	L	P	Y	I	R	U	E	A
M	Y	W	L	A	X	C	V	R
E	T	Q	N	O	N	E	M	E
T	D	C	Q	A	D	U	N	H
T	E	J	D	I	P	U	C	S
R	A	N	E	O	H	U	R	A
D	O	N	N	E	R	R	Q	D
N	E	Z	T	I	L	B	R	U

DASHER
DANCER
PRANCER
VIXEN
COMET
CUPID
DONNER
BLITZEN
RUDOLPH

SANTA'S MAZE

Help Henry find Santa's grotto in the shopping centre so he can make sure he gets everything on his list.

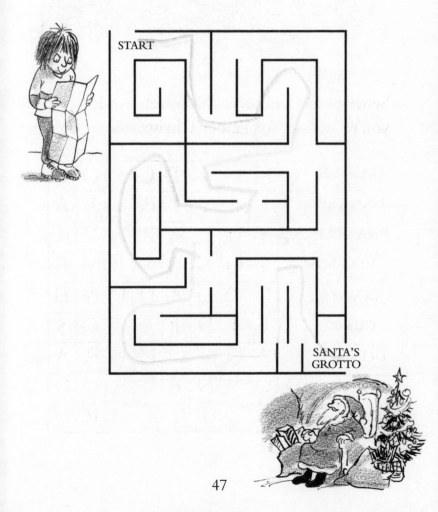

START

SANTA'S
GROTTO

FESTIVE FOOD

It was dark when Henry's family finally sat down to Christmas lunch. Henry's tummy was rumbling so loudly with hunger he thought the walls would cave in. Henry and Peter made a dash to grab the seat against the wall, furthest from the kitchen.

'Get off!' shouted Henry.

'It's my turn to sit here,' wailed Peter.

'Mine!'

'Mine!'

Slap!

Slap!

'WAAAAAA AAAAAAAAA!' screeched Henry.

'WAAAAAA AAAAAAAAA!' wailed Peter.

'Quiet!' screamed Dad.

Find out whether Henry ever gets to eat in 'Horrid Henry's Christmas Lunch' from *Horrid Henry's Christmas Cracker*.

PUNCHLINE CROSS-OUT PUZZLE

Follow the instructions and find the punchline to the joke. Fill in the left-over letters below.

Instructions

Cross out 4 Bs
Cross out 3 Fs
Cross out 5 Hs
Cross out 4 Js
Cross out 3 Ks
Cross out 4 Os
Cross out 3 Ts
Cross out 4 Xs

B	D	J	E	H	O	E
T	F	P	O	A	K	Z
N	B	H	D	J	C	B
K	R	F	O	I	T	C
S	K	P	J	X	A	H
H	N	D	O	E	T	F
V	B	J	E	H	X	N

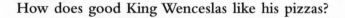

How does good King Wenceslas like his pizzas?

— — — — — — — — — — — — — — — —

HOW TO SURVIVE SPROUTS

Pickles
bread
potatoes
Mincepies
Pud
Choc biscuits
nuts
parsnips
sageand onion
Onions
~~Sprouts~~
crisps

Cross 'sprouts' off Mum's shopping list and write 'crisps' instead.

Hide the bag of sprouts and throw it in the bin when Mum isn't looking.

Sneak the sprouts
off your plate and
into a drawer.

Save them for
your Glop.

Flick them at
Perfect Peter.

GRUESOME GLOP

Horrid Henry and Moody Margaret
love making Christmas Glop.

You will need

a big bowl
a wooden spoon
lots of yucky leftovers
   from Christmas lunch

Instructions

1. Put the leftovers into the
   bowl and mix it all up
   into a gloppy Glop.
2. Invite your friends and
   family to a Glop tasting
   session. (Tee hee!)

**HORRID HENRY'S
GLOP SURPRISE**

Gravy
Brussel sprouts
Stuffing
Mashed Potato
Soup

**MOODY
MARGARET'S
SWEET AND SOUR**

White sauce
Cranberry sauce
Mincemeat
Christmas pudding
Lemonade

CHRISTMAS LUNCH CATASTROPHE

Find the words in the wordsearch. The first five left-over letters spell out Henry's ideal Christmas lunch.

S	S	P	B	I	Z	Y	Z	S	A
A	U	T	R	A	E	K	T	P	P
U	X	T	U	K	C	U	L	R	O
S	H	Y	R	F	N	O	G	O	T
A	K	U	F	T	F	R	N	U	A
G	T	Z	S	A	A	I	B	T	T
E	V	E	R	V	T	Z	N	S	O
S	H	J	Y	P	P	P	G	G	E
C	S	P	I	N	S	R	A	P	S
S	T	O	R	R	A	C	B	F	D

TURKEY   **CARROTS**   **SAUSAGES**
STUFFING   **PARSNIPS**   **CHESTNUTS**
GRAVY   **POTATOES**
SPROUTS   **BACON**

Henry's feast is: __ __ __ __ __

CHRISTMAS DAY DISASTERS

Ding Dong. It must be Rich Aunt Ruby and his horrible cousin. Henry watched as his aunt staggered in carrying boxes and boxes of presents which she dropped under the brightly-lit tree. Most of them, no doubt, for Stuck-up Steve.

'I wish we weren't here,' moaned Stuck-up Steve. 'Our house is so much nicer.'

'Shh,' said Rich Aunt Ruby. She went off with Henry's parents.

Stuck-up Steve looked down at Henry.

'Bet I'll get loads more presents than you,' he said.

'Bet you won't,' said Henry, trying to sound convinced.

'It's not what you get it's the thought that counts,' said Perfect Peter.

'*I'm* getting a Boom-Boom Basher *and a* Goo-Shooter,' said Stuck-up Steve.

'So am I,' said Henry.

What does Horrid Henry get for Christmas? Find out in 'Horrid Henry's Christmas' from *Horrid Henry Gets Rich Quick*.

SPOT THE PAIRS

Mum gives Dad some flowery oven gloves
for Christmas. Find the three matching pairs.

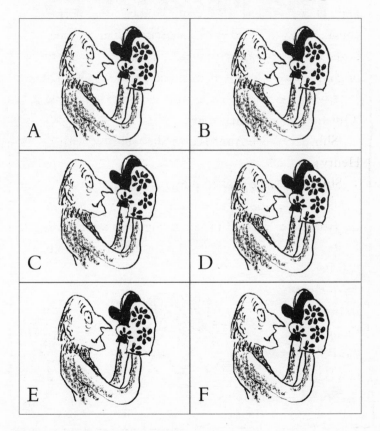

The three pairs are:

__ and __ , __ and __ , __ and __

DO THEY HAVE TO COME? SURVIVING THE RELATIVES

FOR

They give you presents.

They distract Mum and Dad so you can sneak more chocolates off the tree.

It's fun playing pranks on them!

They bring more chocolates!

AGAINST

You have to
give them
presents.

Sharing a bedroom with
Peter – bleccccccch!

Having to be polite.

No TV!

CRAFTY CHRISTMAS CRACKERS

Crackers help Christmas to go with a bang!
Here's how to make your own.

You will need

2 loo rolls

strong glue

piece of crepe paper – big
enough to wrap around
your crackers

cracker 'bang' strip

cracker goodies

paper cut-outs to decorate

Instructions

1. Cut 1 loo roll in half.

2. Using the crepe paper, stick the three cardboard rolls along one side.

3. Holding the centre roll, carefully twist one of the end rolls.

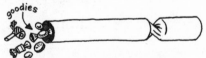

4. Insert the cracker 'bang' strip through the twisted end.

5. Fill the cracker with goodies, like sweets, stickers or a balloon and twist the other end of the tube to contain everything.

6. Stick down both ends of the cracker 'bang' with glue.

7. Decorate the cracker.

It's time to pull your cracker!

SURVIVING THE FAMILY GAMES

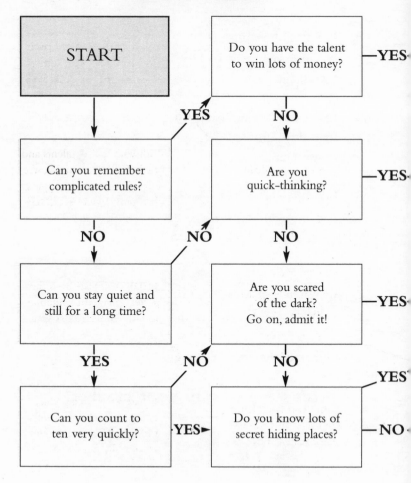

START

Do you have the talent to win lots of money? — **YES**

Can you remember complicated rules?

YES ↑

NO ↓

Are you quick-thinking? — **YES**

NO ↓

NO ↓

Can you stay quiet and still for a long time?

NO ↑

Are you scared of the dark? Go on, admit it! — **YES**

YES ↓

NO ↑

NO ↓

Can you count to ten very quickly?

YES ►

Do you know lots of secret hiding places?

— **YES**

— **NO**

Horrid Henry's top tip for surviving the family games – play a game you're sure to win.

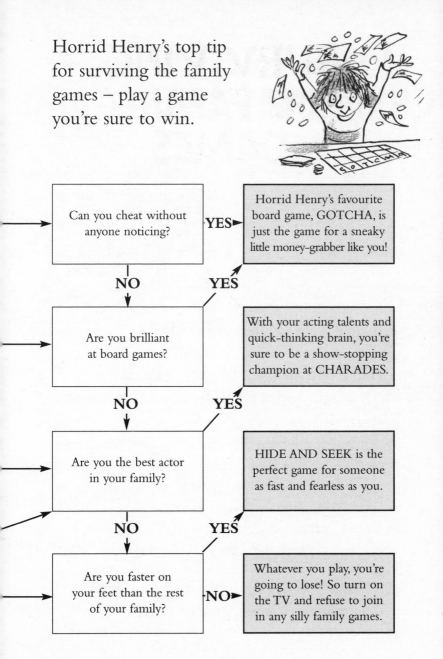

Can you cheat without anyone noticing?

YES► Horrid Henry's favourite board game, GOTCHA, is just the game for a sneaky little money-grabber like you!

NO **YES**

Are you brilliant at board games?

With your acting talents and quick-thinking brain, you're sure to be a show-stopping champion at CHARADES.

NO **YES**

Are you the best actor in your family?

HIDE AND SEEK is the perfect game for someone as fast and fearless as you.

NO **YES**

Are you faster on your feet than the rest of your family?

◄NO► Whatever you play, you're going to lose! So turn on the TV and refuse to join in any silly family games.

FIND THE PAIRS –
CHRISTMAS TEAM GAME

You will need

20 old Christmas cards
scissors
two teams of players

How to play

1. Cut all the Christmas cards in half.
2. Put one batch of halves at one end of the room, and spread them out face-up on the floor.
3. Divide the remaining halves equally between the two teams.
4. Each team member in turn takes half a card, runs to the other end of the room, finds the matching piece and runs back to their team. The first team to complete all their ten cards is the winner.

HENRY'S HOW-TO-WIN TIP

When you divide out the cards, sneak the enemy team an extra card.

Henry

HENRY'S FAMILY CHRISTMAS QUIZ

Can you cope with one final challenge –
Horrid Henry's Family Christmas quiz?

**1. HORRID HENRY asks: Where would I choose
to go for Christmas lunch?**
(a) The Virtuous Veggie
(b) Gobble and Go
(c) Restaurant Le Posh

**2. PERFECT PETER asks:
What starring role did I play
in the school Christmas play?**
(a) Joseph
(b) A blade of grass
(c) The baby Jesus

**3. MUM asks: What did I use to decorate
the table for Christmas lunch?**
(a) Tinsel and baubles
(b) Fresh holly and ivy
(c) Satsumas and walnuts

4. DAD asks: If you bought me a CD for Christmas, what kind of music would I like best?
(a) Pop
(b) Heavy metal
(c) Classical

5. HORRID HENRY asks: What did I tell Father Christmas to give me?

(a) Loads and loads of cash
(b) A skipping rope
(c) Handkerchiefs

6. GRANNY asks: What did Perfect Peter give me for Christmas?
(a) A Mutant Max comic
(b) A skateboard
(c) My favourite perfume

7. PERFECT PETER asks: What did Henry want to put on the top of the Christmas tree?
(a) His teddy, Mr Kill
(b) Terminator Gladiator
(c) A fairy

8. PRISSY POLLY asks: What did Henry's mum and dad give me for Christmas?

(a) A crystal frog vase

(b) A power drill

(c) A pack of dusters

9. PIMPLY PAUL asks: What's the worst Christmas present I've ever received?

(a) A tube of pimple cream

(b) A big box of chocolates

(c) A piece of hairy soap

10. HORRID HENRY asks: In the school Christmas play, I played the innkeeper – what song did I sing?

(a) Silent Night

(b) Ten Green Bottles

(c) We Three Kings

Check out the answers on page 73. Did you do as well as Horrid Henry and his family? Henry gives his verdict:

1-4: Rubbish – this score's as sad as a soggy sprout!

5-7: Not bad – but not brilliant! Like Mum, Dad, Granny, Pimply Paul and Prissy Polly, you'll have to admit that you've been beaten by a better brain.

8-10: Congratulations! A cracking Christmas score. Peter just sneaked in with 8 – but the triumphant winner is ME with 10.

GOODBYE FROM HORRID HENRY

Goodbye, gang! Thanks to my
brilliant guide, I'm sure you'll have
the best Christmas ever - tee hee!

ANSWERS

page 8 Confused Christmas Cards

1. Margaret
2. William
3. Ralph
4. Mrs Oddbod
5. Gurinder
6. Bert

page 9 Christmas Code Message

MEET ME AT THE PURPLE HAND FORT AT NOON!

page 13 Christmas Play Criss-Cross

pages 16-17 Clever Clare's Christmas Quiz

1. (a)
2. (b)
3. (a)
4. (c)
5. (a)
6. (b)

page 19 Puzzling Presents

pages 22–23 Guess the Present

1. Goo-Shooter
2. Catapult
3. Zapatron Hip-Hop Dinosaur
4. Satsuma
5. Bow Tie
6. Socks
7. Terminator Gladiator Trident
8. Dictionary
9. Cello

page 26 Christmas Clockwords

WALNUTS

page 27 What's Inside?

1. DOLL
2. GOO

page 30 Thank You Letter

Dear Aunt Ruby

I do not like my present. It's going in the bin.
Next Christmas, send me money. Send Peter a book. He's a worm.
Henry

page 31 Who Survives the Christmas Crush?

	POSITION IN QUEUE	PRESENTS
HORRID HENRY	1st	CRAYONS
MOODY MARGARET	3rd	SLIME
RUDE RALPH	2nd	SWEETS

page 35 Christmas Tree Wordsearch

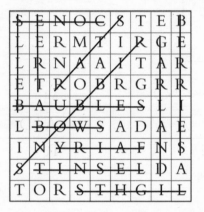

The hidden message is TERMINATOR GLADIATOR

pages 36–37 Spot the Difference

1. Henry has a piece of holly on his head.
2. The star is missing a point.
3. One of the baubles in the box is black.
4. One of the candles on the floor is missing.
5. There's an extra bauble on the tree.
6. The tree has a branch missing.

page 39 Christmas Sudoku

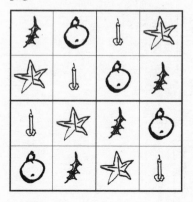

pages 42-43 Criss-Cross Christmas Jokes

1. SOOTS
2. TROUSERS
3. TURKEY
4. TOAD
5. PUDDLE
6. MARY

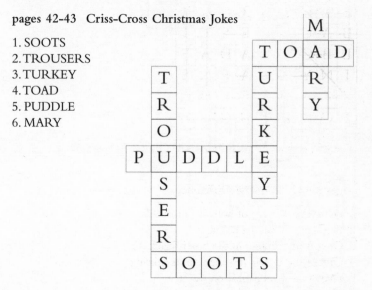

page 46   Santa's Reindeer

page 47   Santa's Maze

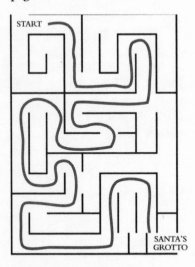

page 49   Punchline Cross-Out Puzzle

DEEP AND CRISP AND EVEN

page 53   Christmas Lunch Catastrophe

Henry's feast is: PIZZA

page 55   Spot the Pairs

The three pairs are:
A and E
B and C (one less petal on middle flower)
D and F (one petal more on top flower)

pages 63–65   Henry's Family Christmas Quiz

1. (b)
2. (a)
3. (b)
4. (c)
5. (a)
6. (c)
7. (b)
8. (a)
9. (c)
10. (b)

More Horrid Henry

Horrid Henry
Horrid Henry and the Secret Club
Horrid Henry Tricks the Tooth Fairy
Horrid Henry's Nits
Horrid Henry Gets Rich Quick
Horrid Henry's Haunted House
Horrid Henry and the Mummy's Curse
Horrid Henry's Revenge
Horrid Henry and the Bogey Babysitter
Horrid Henry's Stinkbomb
Horrid Henry's Underpants
Horrid Henry Meets the Queen
Horrid Henry and the Mega-Mean Time Machine
Horrid Henry and the Football Fiend
Horrid Henry's Christmas Cracker
Horrid Henry and the Abominable Snowman
Horrid Henry Robs the Bank
Horrid Henry Wakes the Dead
Horrid Henry Rocks

For a complete list of **Horrid Henry** titles,
visit **www.horridhenry.co.uk**